For Bryson,

Dream Big!

Enjoy the adventure,

Susanne

Busker the Tusker & Friends™

Series

For my husband, Hayden.
You inspire me.
Thank you for your unconditional love, support
and for believing in a dream you helped me turn into reality.

ISBN: 978-0-578-40137-9

Library of Congress Control Number: 2018913662

Printed and bound in the United States of America
First printing, June 2019

Published by Susie's Stories, Inc
Little Rock, Arkansas

Summary: Asleep at an oasis, a young elephant named Busker wakes up to find his family gone. He sets out on an adventure to find them and meets unlikely friends who possess skills that may help spot his herd through Africa's various habitats.

Busker the Tusker and Friends Series

Busker the Tusker

by Susanne Brunner

Illustrated by Wynter Bresaw

Illustration edits by Xavier Moncayo

SUSIE'S STORIES INC.

It was a hot day across the Sahara Desert. Three pillow-shaped clouds floated in the light blue sky. Underneath a shaded tree, fast asleep, was Busker the Tusker.

Busker the Tusker is an African Bush Elephant with ivory tusks and is the youngest of the herd. He slept through the loud sounds of the African wilderness.

Z Z Z Z Z . . .

Not even the sound of elephants bathing in the cool oasis could bring this Tusker to his feet.

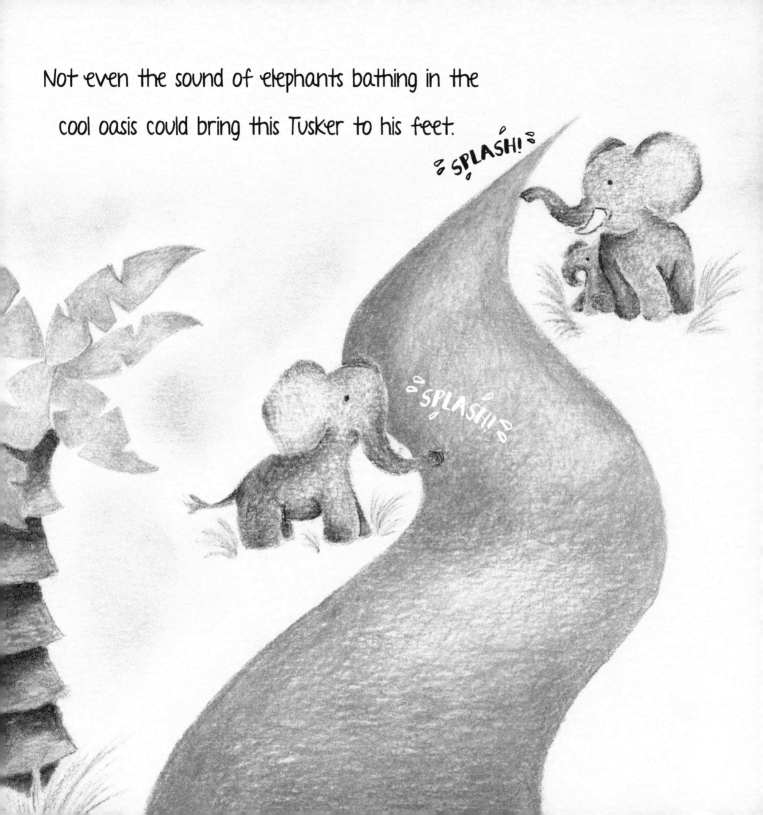

Coming from his long gray trunk

was a snore so loud.

So loud, Busker woke up.

Busker looked around the oasis.

"Where did everyone go?"

His eyes filled with tears.

He wiped away the tears with his trunk
to make sure it wasn't a dream.

Busker's family was gone!

Busker grabbed his blue backpack that was filled with all sorts of handy items. He pulled out the magnifying glass to search for any clues.

Busker found animal tracks in the sand!

te followed them for a while until they disappeared.

Then, a gold paw magnified before his eyes.

Busker raised his magnifying glass to get a closer look.

"Hi, I'm Loren the Roarin' Lion.
Are you lost?"

"Yes," Busker replied.
"I can't find my family.
Have you seen them?"

Loren let out a big roar, "I haven't seen
any elephants, but they might be in the
rainforest. I can help you find them."

CHIRP CHIRP!

CHIRP CHIRP!

Busker the Tusker gladly accepted.
He knew with Loren the Roarin' Lion's
powerful roar, his family could hear him.

Sand turned into big trees and plants.
The animals that lived here brought this
rainforest to life.

Before Busker could take another step, a banana fell before him.

A monkey was swinging from branch to branch toward them, then slid down a long vine.

The monkey fixed her banana skirt and asked, "What brings an elephant and lion to my rainforest?"

"I can't find my family. Have you seen them?" asked Busker.

"Not around here. But I can go with you to look for them," she offered.

"My name is Mizzy,"
said the monkey.

Busker thanked her. He was excited to have two friends helping with the search. He knew with Mizzy the Monkey's acrobatic skills across the rainforest, she could help him spot his herd.

Busker looked around with his magnifying glass to find clues while Mizzy raced ahead swinging from tree to tree to find the elephants.

Loren let out a loud roar.
Animals ran up the trees and clung
to branches as the sound rattled pieces
of fruit and leaves to the ground.

ROAR

Still, no elephants were in sight.

Busker the Tusker, Loren the Roarin' Lion and Mizzy the Monkey walked out the other side of the rainforest.

Right in front of them was the longest river in the world--

the Nile River.

All three raced to the river to get a drink.
Busker gulped the water through his trunk. His reflection
faded away as he noticed something in the water.

It was Kyle the Crocodile of the Nile.

All of the animals knew Kyle.

He had ruled these waters for years.

"Hi Kyle, have you seen Busker's herd of elephants?" asked Mizzy.

"I've been up and down the Nile all day, but haven't seen them," said Kyle. "What happened?"

"I was sleeping at the oasis and when I woke up my family was gone," Busker explained.

"Cheer up Busker, we will find them. I, Kyle the Crocodile of the Nile, will keep watch along these waters."

Busker the Tusker, Loren the Roarin' Lion and Mizzy the Monkey went on their way. A sound in the distance caught Busker's attention.

Two hyenas were sitting on the sand dunes laughing.

Busker looked down with sadness.

Mizzy patted him and said, "Don't worry about them. They are not making fun of you. That's how they are with everyone."

Loren let out a roar. The hyenas scattered.

Soon, the brown sand turned into green grass as they entered the savanna. Herds of animals were all over the land, but the elephants were nowhere to be found.

Busker felt a gust of wind and something land on his back.

It was Sully the Woolly-necked Stork, the best guide in the savanna.

"Well look who we have here!

What is an elephant doing

without his herd?"

"We are looking for my family," said Busker. "Have you seen them?"

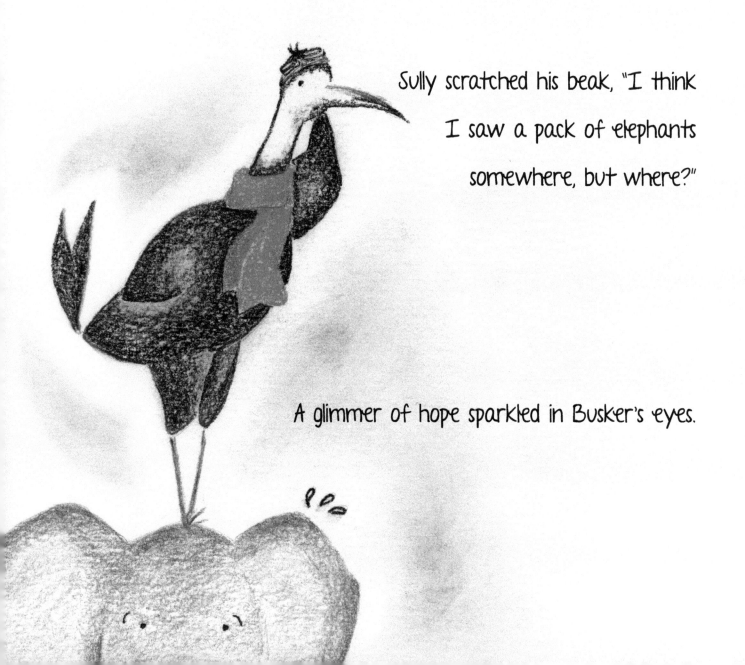

Sully scratched his beak, "I think
I saw a pack of elephants
somewhere, but where?"

A glimmer of hope sparkled in Busker's eyes.

Sully took flight and shouted from the sky, "I'll be back, Busker. I'm going to help you find your family!"

With Sully the Woolly-necked Stork's aerial view, Busker knew he would find the elephants in no time.

Sully disappeared in the distance. Busker the Tusker, Loren the Roarin' Lion and Mizzy the Monkey passed herds of giraffes, zebras and hippos while they kept searching for clues.

After walking for some time, they came upon sand once again.

CAW CAW!

Sully the Woolly-necked Stork was circling in the sky far ahead.

Did the best guide in the savanna find something?

Mizzy hopped on Loren's back and clung onto his long golden hair.

They ran fast toward Sully.

As they got closer, Busker saw a familiar place and heard a familiar sound.

Then, Busker felt a gallon of water splash on his face!

"Busker!

Busker!

BUSKER, WAKE UP!"

Busker slowly lifted his eyelids. The sight of his mother came in clear. He looked around and noticed he was lying underneath the same tree at the oasis.

"Where have you been mama? I've been looking for you."

"Busker, I haven't gone anywhere and neither have you.
We've been at the oasis the whole time," his mother said.

"But, you and the herd were gone when I woke up!

I met a lion, monkey, crocodile and stork

who all helped me find you."

"That must have been some dream, Busker.

We would never leave our little Tusker behind! Families leave no

one behind," his mother said as she patted his head.

"Come on, it's time to go back to the savanna."

Busker the Tusker got to his feet and put on his blue backpack. He grabbed onto his mother's tail with his trunk and followed the herd out of the oasis.

A golden glow in the distance caught Busker's attention.

It was a lion. It looked at the elephants, let out a loud roar, and ran toward the rainforest.

"Do you know who that is, Busker?" his mother asked.

"That's Loren the Roarin' Lion. He will be the king of his pride one day."

Busker nodded knowingly and looked back to where Loren was. The Tusker gripped his mother's tail, focusing on another long journey ahead.

About the Author

Susanne Brunner is an Emmy award-winning news anchor.
While anchoring the morning news in Little Rock, Arkansas, Susanne shares
weekly education reports. Some have highlighted positive stories about the
importance of reading at an early age, and ensuring more kids have
a book of their own.

Susanne's goal is to write stories that teach kids important life lessons. She also
hopes her books help build a special bond between children and their parents.
Growing up, Susanne's mom told her a special, favorite bedtime story that she
remembers and holds dear to this day. That memory encouraged Susanne to
create a tale of her own to tell, which is how Busker the Tusker came to life.

In addition to reading books in elementary classrooms, Susanne has volunteered her time through Junior Achievement to help
students learn about financial literacy, job readiness and entrepreneurship. The state has recognized Susanne for her efforts
helping hundreds of unemployed Arkansans find work through career fairs she has hosted and promoted.

Susanne is from Placerville, California. Her father served 22 years in the United States Air Force. As a "military brat,"
she moved with her family to many bases throughout California and her mother's home country--the Philippines.

A graduate of Yuba College with an A.S. in Mass Communications, Susanne also attended San Francisco State University where
she earned a B.A. in Radio and Television with an emphasis in Broadcast Journalism.

Susanne resides in the Little Rock area with her husband, Hayden.

CPSIA information can be obtained
at www.ICGtesting.com
Printed in the USA
LVHW011037050719
623205LV00004B/7/P